Amish Romance
Faith Alone

Grace Given

Clean Christian Romance

PUREREAD.COM

Copyright © 2016 by **Grace Given**

All rights reserved. No part of this publication may be reproduced, distributed or transmitted in any form or by any means, without prior written permission.

Grace Given/PureRead Ltd
www.pureread.com

Publisher's Note: This is a work of fiction. Names, characters, places, and incidents are a product of the author's imagination. Locales and public names are sometimes used for atmospheric purposes. Any resemblance to actual people, living or dead, or to businesses, companies, events, institutions, or locales is completely coincidental.

This book is dedicated to YOU - the reader!
It is your encouragement and friendship, your emails, feedback and reviews, that make every one of these books so special!

NEVER MISS A NEW STORY
Want to be notified other Amish romance and mysteries by Grace Given? Sign up for New Releases and receive a free novella as a reward.

www.pureread.com/gracegiven

"For we walk by faith, not by sight"

2 Corinthians 5:7

A PERSONAL WORD FROM GRACE

Angels Among Us charts the history of the beautiful adventurous soul of Rebekah . Hers is a walk of faith not only in what she sees, but in the invisible truths that sustain every pilgrim through life.

"Rebekah Stoltzfus, who for so long resisted the idea of marriage, discovers the sheer joy of companionship with her childhood sweetheart and best friend, Eli Stauffer. All is well in her world and she has so much to thank her Gott for. But will she continue to offer up praise when her world crashes around her? Having our faith tested like this can break us or make us. Will Rebekah allow the questions she faces to find their answer in the providence of her Gott?"

Grace Given, Author

Contents

Life Within 1
The Right Man 9
Jacob Byler 15
Warm Companions 21
The Accident 27
Faith Alone 37
Strength to Live 45
The Father's Arms 51
Awakening 57
Read Them All 61
Bonus Chapter – Love's Promise 63

CHAPTER ONE

Life Within

REBEKAH STAUFFER FELT the movement of life within her and smiled. When Eli came through the kitchen door he caught his breath when he looked at his wife. Motherhood only enhanced her beauty. Both of them eagerly anticipated the birth of their first child. Eli gazed at Rebekah until she looked up at him.

"It will not be long now, Eli," she said.

"Are you sure, Rebekah? I thought the boppli would not arrive until early summer."

"I do not think he or she knows that," said Rebekah. "Perhaps the boppli does not realize late spring is not early summer."

They laughed and Eli agreed she could be right. The young Amish couple had taken the advice of Clara Stoltzfus, Rebekah's mother, and arranged for the birth to be in the local Englisch hospital.

Both Clara and Eli's mother felt it best for Rebekah to take no chances in case something did not go right. Ruby Stauffer reassured her daughter-in-law that nothing would go wrong but felt it best. The nearest Amish midwife was eight miles away. They lined up their Englisch friend, Danny Combs, to take them in his car when the time came.

That night when Rebekah rested her head on the down pillow she felt more movement than usual. In the middle of the night, she nudged Eli and told him she felt it was time. Eli quickly pulled on his clothes and raced to the barn. He had everything ready including the saddle hanging over the stall gate to throw on his horse. He sped to Danny's house which was the first Englisch one at the edge of Amish land. Danny and his wife had retired. He told Eli he would be right there.

"I will ride back to Rebekah," said Eli. "We will be ready."

On the fast ride home, Eli prayed all would go well with Rebekah and their newborn. Without rubbing down his horse as usual, he raced to the house just as Danny drove up.

"I am ready," said his wife. Her serenity surprised Eli. "Do not worry so, Eli. Everything will be fine and we will soon be hearing cries of a boppli keeping us awake at night."

Danny took Rebekah's overnight bag and placed it next to her in the back seat. Eli spent most of the ride to the hospital looking back at her. Her sudden sharp cry alarmed him.

"We are just a block away," said Danny. "Hang in there Rebekah."

This was not Danny Combs' first time to take a soon-to-be Amish mother to the community hospital. He held a good report with his Amish neighbors and though he doubted he could live such simple lives as they did, he admired them. Swerving under the canopy that sheltered the emergency room entrance, he braked and jumped out. Then he followed Eli and Rebekah through the doorway. Once they were greeted by the receptionist, he told them he hoped everything would go as expected and left.

"I will let your families know you are here," said Danny.

Eli nodded and thanked him, then turned to his wife. A nurse appeared and settled Rebekah into a wheelchair and rolled her to the maternity ward with Eli on their heels.

Word spread around the Amish community that Bishop Daniel and Clara Stoltzfus welcomed their grandson the next afternoon. Ruby and Robert Stauffer waited with them in the small room off the ward. When the nurse told them they could go into Rebekah's room, they hurried to see their new grandson. Eli smiled broadly and stood in wonder as he gazed on his small son. Rebekah fought to keep her eyes open but greeted her visitors with more happiness than she could remember ever feeling.

"Let us bow our heads in thanksgiving for this new boppli who has joined us all," said Bishop Stoltzfus.

He prayed aloud and praised their Gott for His blessings on their family. When he finished, everyone's face displayed smiles all around.

Two days later Rebekah and Eli once again rode in Danny's car back to their home. Their parents had spent the last few hours preparing everything for their arrival. Neighbors continued to arrive with food and when the Stauffers came in with their child, no one could wait to have a look at the fair child.

"He has his Daed's fair skin and light hair," said one woman.

Clara and Ruby settled Rebekah in the rocker in the bedroom and placed the baby in her arms. The rest of the women served everyone food and after a short nap, Rebekah took Eli's hand. He brought her into the kitchen where her best friend, Nancy Yoder handed her a plate of food. Eli's best friend, Jacob Byler, stood at the doorway and beamed at the happiness surrounding him.

After two hours passed, the women began to gather their dishes, now empty, and pack them into their buggies. The icebox was filled in Rebekah's kitchen and a cake and pie were set on the counter.

"It is time for the three of you to become better acquainted," said Clara. She kissed her daughter. "Get some rest and I will be back when you need me." Her eyes twinkled. "Or I will be back when you want me as well."

"You are welcome to come over every day if you wish," said Rebekah.

The house restored to peace and calm once again and only Eli and Rebekah sat in the living room. The baby slept in a small bed in his bedroom. It separated his parent's room and the sitting room.

"We must think about a name for our boppli," said Eli.

Rebekah agreed and they talked of names already thought about. They prepared for either a boy or a girl and now sifted through several boys' names. Among them were Jacob, Eli, Daniel and Robert. Rebekah suggested they have Jacob's name in it and Eli agreed it was a fine idea.

"We can use your Daadi's first name. He meant a lot to you before he went on to his reward," said Eli.

Rebekah's eyes misted when she thought of her beloved grandfather. "That is a gut idea, Eli. Danka, for thinking of that. Samuel Jacob it is."

During the night Samuel awakened his parents several times. Eli brought him to his mother each time. The new father did not complain about interrupted sleep even though spring was well along in its season, and much work waited for him. His days were long ones but his contentment overrode any inconvenience. Each morning he prayed aloud with his wife and again each evening. Samuel felt their ease and in a matter of weeks, he slept most of the night. Rebekah returned to her household duties with Samuel always nearby. He was a happy child and she was astounded at his resemblance to his father.

One morning when the sun shone bright over the foliage that emerged, Rebekah heard the clip-clop of horses' hooves on the dirt lane. She glanced up to see Jacob Byler drive up. When he jumped from the buckboard, his eyes went to the child wrapped and sleeping in the large basket.

"How is Samuel?" said Jacob. His eyes glistened in the sunlight. Jacob had truly become attached to the baby and every chance that came along, he visited. Before he greeted either Rebekah or Eli, he first reached for Samuel.

Rebekah laughed. "He is just fine as always, Jacob. What brings you out today?"

"Eli told me he has extra fence poles I can use until the store gets more in. I have several posts that need replacing. I will go and get them."

He started for the barn and then remembered his wagon.

"I wondered if you were going to haul them by hand from the barn to the wagon," said Rebekah.

The childhood friends could not resist teasing each other as they did when young. Jacob, Eli, Rebekah and Nancy Yoder were lifelong friends and they knew each other as if siblings. Jacob felt a faint flush to his cheeks. He often forced his feelings for Rebekah away. He did not resent his best friend marrying her but he could not help old feelings for her surfacing sometimes. He climbed back onto the wagon and ordered his horses to go toward the barn. He loaded several posts in the back and stopped to tell Rebekah to let Eli know he got them. After he left, Rebekah smiled to herself thinking how blessed she was in her life with family and good friends. Samuel drifted off to sleep again as she continued to weed the garden. There would be plenty of canned vegetables once winter came around again. For now, winter was far away. Spring and summer were Rebekah's favorite times of the year.

"They are my favorite unless you count fall, too, Samuel," she said.

His eyes fluttered and then shut again. Rebekah gathered her tools and placed the small pile of weeds in her apron. She took them to the barrel where they would dry out and later be burned. Across the field she saw Eli behind the horse and plow. The crops looked good so far.

Rebekah looked up at the cobalt blue skies and scooped up Samuel in his basket. Everything was right in their world and she whispered a prayer of praise.

CHAPTER TWO

The Right Man

NANCY YODER ENVIED her best friend. When those feelings rose up within her, she prayed for strength to not feel that way. She did not wish to be married to Eli. She only desired to marry the man she had always loved and to have a family of her own. Jacob Byler showed no interest in her beyond friendship. Once that had been enough for her, but now she decided she and Jacob would never be a couple. It was hard for Nancy to draw other men in the community to her. It dawned on her that there was only one person to talk things over with and that was Rebekah herself.

It was Sunday afternoon and no services were held that week. The in between Sundays were meant for family and for visiting friends. She hitched the horse to the open buggy and headed for the Stauffer home. When she arrived Rebekah and Eli sat on the porch with Samuel on her lap.

"Look at my Samuel," said Nancy. "He is a fine boppli for sure."

Often Rebekah and Eli talked of how Samuel seemed to belong to everyone and they happily accepted that. Eli stood and offered Nancy his chair.

"While the two of you visit, I will go to my parents' haus and see how they are getting along." Eli looked at their son.

"Go ahead and take Samuel with you. His Daadi and Grohs-mammi will want to see him, too," said Rebekah.

She went inside to pack a small cloth bag with things Samuel may need and handed it and Samuel to her husband. It was hard to let go of her boppli but she knew how much Samuel meant to her husband too. Once the two were settled in the buggy, Eli drove off slowly.

"He is a gut daed, Rebekah," said Nancy.

"Ja, he is that. Sometimes I think he is reluctant to work in the fields when he looks at him in the morning." The women remained silent for a few seconds. "What is going on in your life, Nancy?" asked Rebekah.

"I have not visited lately. Spring is a busy time for everyone," said Nancy. "I do want to talk to you about something, Rebekah. You are my best friend and you are always here for me."

Rebekah looked quickly at her friend. She waited for her to go on.

Nancy continued. "You and Eli are so happy together. Did you ever think when we were children that you would marry him?"

Rebekah shook her head no. "I did not think about marriage then. The truth of the matter is I did not want to marry anyone until two years ago. One day when Eli stopped at my haus something hit me that was different about him." She laughed. "I suppose there was nothing different about him. It was me. I suddenly looked at him in a different way. He wanted to court me long before I allowed him to do so. Now I realize I wasted time with my stubbornness."

"You are very lucky. The man I wish would court me treats me like his little shveshtah. I have been in love with Jacob for a very long time."

Rebekah jerked her head toward her best friend. "I did not know you have had Jacob in mind all this time. Why did you keep that from me?"

"I thought perhaps you would think me foolish. We have all been gut friends for a long time and you may think that it is silly of me. Then when you and Eli fell in love, I wanted to tell you but could not bring myself to do so."

"Jacob is a fine man. I know everything happens at the right time. Maybe it is a matter of him clicking with you as I did with Eli."

Rebekah attempted to encourage her friend but she knew Jacob put off the advances Nancy made toward him. She also knew that Jacob began to notice Marian Zook as of late. The young widow had asked the community for help with painting her house. The paint was chipping on the backside of it. Marian's husband died of a terminal illness over a year ago. She was left with two young children to raise on her own. Marian started her basket shop several years before her husband passed away. Now it paid off for her to have it. Otherwise, she had no way of making a living on her own. The community was always there for her but she did not often ask for help.

Nancy twirled the tip of a stick on the board plank of the porch. "I know Jacob offered to paint Marian's house, along with others. I believe he is showing an interest in her," she said.

Rebekah breathed a sigh of relief that her friend was aware of this. "He does seem interested in her. I would not let that deter you though. Perhaps it would be gut if you had a talk with Jacob. If he is not interested in you in that way, you would be free to search elsewhere. I know plenty of young men who want to court you."

Rebekah looked at Nancy and her beauty stood out. She was kind and helpful as well. Nancy possessed all the necessary skills to run a household. And she would make a wonderful mother and wife. She told Nancy her thoughts. A slight flush covered Nancy's face.

"I know several men have asked to court me. I am not getting any younger," she said. "You are right in that I should go elsewhere. I may as well admit to myself that Jacob likes me very much but not in that way."

Her hands fell to her lap and the stick toppled onto the floor. Rebekah patted her hand.

"The right man is out there. The day may come that Jacob will look at you as you do him, but do not count on that. You are missing the man you are meant to have," said Rebekah.

Nancy Yoder thanked her friend and stood to go just as Eli and Samuel came toward the house. On her way home, she knew Rebekah was right. She also was well aware that Jacob Byler had always hoped Rebekah would be his one day and was disappointed when Rebekah chose Eli. To this day, she was sure neither Eli nor Rebekah sensed this fact. She prayed Jacob and Marian would find love between them and then she prayed Gott would lead her to the right partner in life. Her shoulders sank at the thought that Jacob would never be hers.

Rebekah stood to take Samuel from Eli. "Did he enjoy his visit with his Daaed and Grohsmammi?"

Eli laughed. "He tried to talk with them but of course, he is still too small for that. Ja, he should sleep well tonight. With everyone giving him attention, there was no nap for him."

They walked inside the house. Once Samuel was settled in his crib, Rebekah went to the stove to prepare supper. Warm air seeped through the gauze curtains and she breathed in the summer air. Eli left to milk the cows before time to eat. He smiled when he imagined Samuel one day walking with him to do chores. He recalled how small he was when his daed handed him the pail and showed him how to milk. It was several years later when he knew how to do that on his own. The smell of fresh hay brought back fond memories of when he and his brothers learned farming. That was something Eli cherished and thought back on with happiness. He looked forward to teaching his young son everything his own daed taught him. He praised Gott for giving him a healthy son.

CHAPTER THREE

Jacob Byler

JACOB BYLER WAS WELCOMED at Marian Zook's home when he came to assess the job of painting.

"Come in, Jacob. I am sure you are very busy with your own work. I want you to know how much I appreciate your time. New paint on my haus was never something I thought of when Abram was alive. He took care of things like that."

Jacob assured her he had time to look at the job and that he had several men lined up to get it done. Marian invited him to have a cup of coffee. Her two young daughters played together on the porch. Jacob's smile in their direction warmed Marian. Abram often gave attention to the girls before he did her. He was so happy with his family. She tried not to think about the day the Doctor at the hospital in town told them there was no hope for him. They had long talks together and through her own tears she tried to comfort him as best she could. He made her promise she would one day remarry and find a good father for their children. "You must be happy above all, Marian," he had said. When he took his last breath, she could think of nothing except that Abram was the perfect man for her and now their Gott had taken him away from her.

"This kaffe is gut, Marian. Danka."

Jacob sipped it while Marian set a plate of fresh oatmeal cookies in front of him. They talked a while and then went outside to look at the house. Jacob was surprised the paint was chipped as badly as it was. He knew Abram would never have let it get this bad but did not fault Marian. She had her hands full taking care of two children under age five plus the few animals they had. A neighbor farmed the small field of alfalfa for her. Besides, the chores necessary at home, Marian made baskets and sold them in her store. Her sister took care of the girls during the daytime and helped when Marian was busy in the store.

"We will get this taken care of tomorrow," said Jacob. "I know how much paint it will take and will purchase it before we come out again."

"There is paint in the storage shed. I am not sure if it is what you will need or not," said Marian. Jacob followed her to the shed. Several buckets of paint were sealed and placed in the corner of the structure. "Abram bought it a few months before he became ill and never was well enough to use it. I am sure it is for the haus."

Jacob thanked her and told her they could get started sooner than expected since the paint was already purchased. As he drove away, he thought about Marian Zook. She was pretty and very adept at taking over whatever needed to be done to keep her family fed and safe. He thought of her two daughters and realized he truly loved children. He wanted some of his own. However, when he thought of Marian and her girls he wondered if he may be able to love the woman if he got to know her better. He wanted to marry and settle down. Hannah and Ruth were children with good dispositions like their mother. A sense of peace enveloped him when he thought about them becoming his family. As much as he thought about it, something held him back from pursuing Marian Zook. He liked her a lot but did not know if he could come to love her or not.

Marian went inside when he left and began to prepare the evening meal. She thought about Jacob and wondered if she read him right. Was he showing an interest in her above painting the house for her? She shook her head and thoughts of Abram flooded her heart and mind. "Oh, Abram, how I still miss you," she said aloud. The children looked her way and she told the four year old Hannah she could set the table. The child reached for the top plate and slid it in place for her mother. Then she placed the other two for herself and her three year old sister Ruth. They bowed their heads while Marian gave thanks for the food. She focused on her children and their activities. Her heart sank thinking that Abram would not be around to see them grow up. She wondered if either of her daughters would remember what he looked like.

In the Stauffer household, Eli told Rebekah he would be at Marian Zook's home the next morning to repaint her house. Rebekah had prepared food for the painters as had other women whose husbands planned to work on the house. Rebekah's mother would stop and pick her up with Samuel. The baby would join other little ones and be taken care of by a few of the older girls.

"I believe we will have seven or eight on the paint job. We should be finished soon enough," said Eli. "Jacob told me there were a few other chores needed around the barn, too."

"It must be very hard for Marian to keep things going so well without Abram. I feel sad for her at times," said Rebekah.

Eli leaned over her and kissed her lightly on her forehead. Familiar warmth filtered through her and she smiled up at her husband. She vowed to visit Marian more often to help where needed. The young girls were growing fast and were very active. She was sure all of Marian's energies were spent by the end of a day. She decided to inquire among the women in regard to someone taking care of the evening milking for Marian. That would relieve her some. Rebekah could not imagine her life without Eli.

The next day everyone involved arrived at the Zook house. Marian's sister took the girls to the shop. She planned to keep it open that day for Marian. The men got busy right away and Marian made a large urn of hot coffee and a three gallon jug of lemonade. Women arrived and helped arrange food on two long tables set up outside. Then they sat down and visited until the men took a break for lunch.

"They are doing a gut job of it," said Marian. "I am so grateful for everyone helping out."

The women assured her she would do the same for any of them if needed. Marian poured glasses of lemonade and thanked her Gott for good neighbors. The men sat down and the women dished out plates of roast chicken and beef stew. Large bowls of slaw and potato salad were placed in the middle of the tables along with fresh bread and newly churned butter. Pickled beets and salad greens added to the spread. Coffee cups were refilled before the men got back to the job. By early afternoon, the house looked new on all sides. Eli and Jacob, along with the Brenneman brothers worked in the barn repairing stalls.

"We had better check the fences to make sure none need repair," said Jacob.

The men walked the perimeter of the pasture and met again satisfied that the fencing was in excellent repair. One of the brothers offered to come each evening and milk the two cows for Marian. Rebekah heard him offer, and spoke up.

"I will help you churn some of the milk for butter," she said. "Fall will come around before we know it and then winter again. It will get you ahead on some of the preserving."

Marian smiled and thanked her for her generosity. "Sometimes it is hard to keep up with everything. I could not do it at all without gut friends like all of you." She sliced large pieces of chocolate cake and lemon pie and set them down before the stragglers who remained. Rebekah poured more coffee. They all enjoyed the delicious sweets. Before leaving, everyone told Marian to let them know when they could help out.

Jacob lingered longer than anyone. He told himself that he wanted to update Marian on things that had been done. In fact, he wanted to get to know her better.

CHAPTER FOUR

Warm Companions

REBEKAH SWADDLED SAMUEL and gazed lovingly on his face as he went to sleep. Eli rested his hand on her shoulder and his heart filled with love for his family.

"He will grow fast, Rebekah," said Eli. "I have already thought about things I can teach him to do. When he walks, he can follow me to the barn and I will show him where to place the pail for each cow."

Rebekah laughed. "That is gut planning, Eli, but look at him. He is yet a boppli. There will be plenty of time."

They returned to the living room and visited over cups of hot tea. Rebekah told her husband of the upcoming summer picnic hosted by everyone in their community.

"The Bylers have offered their yard for it all."

"It will be a gut break for us all," said Eli. "Right now things are in place before harvesting time that will come all too soon. What are you going to cook for the event?"

Rebekah mentioned potato salad, slaw and roasted corn. She and her mother planned to cut up a variety of vegetables to add to a stew. Clara's stew was always a success and more than once she willingly handed her recipe over to anyone who asked for it.

Eli then picked up the Bible and began reading from a Psalm. The joyful message helped end their day with peace in their hearts.

The next morning Rebekah rushed to complete her own home tasks. Then she readied Samuel for the short trip to her parents' home. When they arrived, Clara reached for her grandson. She then took him to her husband's small office. Lately, the Bishop was dealing with a community member who drew away from the community. He prayed much about the young teen in hopes he would not decide to go and live in the outside world. When he saw his grandson, Daniel beamed.

"He is a fine lad, Clara," he said.

His wife agreed and then took him to the nook near the kitchen. She had a cradle ready for him and once he was fed, he curled up and slept peacefully. Rebekah and Clara began preparation for the next day's picnic. They chatted about their neighbors and the generosity of the Bylers to provide space for the get-together.

"I do wish Jacob would show some interest in a young woman. He would be a gut catch for someone," said Clara.

"I did notice he seems to take an interest in Widow Zook," said Rebekah. "She is a fine woman and I am sure she wishes to find someone as gut as Abram was to her and her small ones."

Clara raised her eyebrows in response to the news. "I'm sure she does, too. It will all be in Gott's gut time."

Both women worked in silence for a few minutes. Each wondered what it would be like for them if their husbands were no longer around. Rebekah shook her head to rid it of such thoughts. Abram battled a debilitating illness. Eli was strong and healthy. They would have a long life together.

Picnic day arrived bringing plenty of sunshine and a soft cool breeze added to the comfort of everyone. Some spread blankets on the grass and most of the elders opted to sit at the tables set up for the occasion. Young girls poured drinks for everyone and assisted at the two long tables laden with food. Once they finished their meal, games began. Children were separated for games according to ages. The adults chose horseshoe games, sack races and other amusements. Laughter filled the air.

The men discussed the progression of their crops and exchanged tips including nursing sick animals. The women talked of sewing and knitting projects they worked on. Clara mentioned she was sure her garden would provide much more than she and the Bishop would consume over the winter months. She offered to share with others. In what seemed to be too short a time, evening edged over the horizon. Things were collected and placed in buggies. The boys quickly dismantled the tables while others took care in leaving the lawn as they found it. The buggies rolled away to respective homes. Rebekah pointed out the long line of them on the curve.

"They are pretty as they move against the sunset," she said.

Eli agreed it was quite a sight. Then he told her of news Jacob and Isaac mentioned. "There will be a wedding in late Fall of this season," he said. "Did you know that Martha Herschberger will marry Mark Lapp soon?"

Rebekah freed her hands from under Samuel and clapped. "I had not heard it would be this season. I am very happy for them. If they are as happy as we are, it will be a gut marriage." She wrapped one hand around Eli's arm and the other cradled Samuel.

"That is true, my Fraa," said Eli. That night the Stauffer family slept soundly after their active day.

The next morning arrived as bright as the one before. It was Sunday and church services would be held at the Yoder home. Once again everyone brought enough food to serve after the service. Bishop Stoltzfus stood before his congregation to bring them to attention. The men sat on one side of the room and the women on the other. Nancy sat next to Rebekah. She leaned over and whispered to her.

"I am sure I have lost Jacob to Marian Zook," she said.

Rebekah squeezed her hand in comfort and whispered back. "We will talk later. As you look at the men, do you see anyone you could become interested in?"

The entire whispered conversation went on as both women focused their eyes on the Bishop as he spoke. After a long discourse, everyone stood and sang a hymn. It was nearly as long as the sermon had been since every verse was sung. Once seated again, the Bishop introduced a Preacher from a nearby community who then preached a lengthy sermon. Before services ended another Preacher stood and gave his message and more hymns were sung. After several hours, everyone assembled for the dinner. Tables were set up and the food presented in abundance. Rebekah had a chance to speak with Nancy privately once the adults wrapped up the day and left the young ones to gather.

"I am sure you will find the person that will reach your heart, Nancy," said Rebekah. "Let us pray that the person will find you and you will connect right away." They walked a short distance from the others and bowed their heads in prayer.

"Danka, Rebekah, you know how to make me feel better about things. Prayer is the best recourse of all," said Nancy.

The two friends walked back and joined the others on the grass. Rebekah sat with Eli who held Samuel. They talked a few minutes and then left the unmarried ones to the afternoon and evening. On the way home, Rebekah thought of the days when she and Eli stayed and talked with others. They stayed for the sing which lasted until around nine or ten in the evening. She enjoyed that time, but was much more content with her life than she could have imagined at the time.

CHAPTER FIVE

The Accident

REBEKAH FINISHED THE early morning chores in the house and placed Samuel in his basket. She lifted it and took him to the garden. She prepared to plant a late summer crop of radishes and carrots in the garden. When Rebekah started for the small tool shed to retrieve tools, she saw Eli stop his weeding in the nearby field. She watched as he bent to look at the horse's shoe then he unhitched it from the plow and walked it back to the barn.

He saw Rebekah and they met at the gate.

"I will have to stop work and go to the blacksmith's in town. The shoe needs repairing," said Eli.

"Is there not an extra one here?" asked Rebekah. She knew Eli was almost finished with weeding fields and did not want to spare the time to go to town.

"I gave it to my daed when he needed one. It will not take long and I will return soon. Do you need anything from the store?"

Rebekah mentioned several needed items to Eli. He kissed his wife on the forehead and then did the same to his son. Eli hitched the second horse to the buggy and waved as he started for the lane from their house. Rebekah's heart lurched slightly. She placed her hand on it and wondered what had disturbed her. She watched Eli's buggy until it was out of sight and then returned to her planting.

When Eli arrived in the small town, he saw several Englischers he knew and stopped for a short conversation before walking across the road to the Blacksmith Shop. Inside the shop were two customers ahead of him. One was Mark Lapp and the other was someone who appeared familiar to Eli but he could not place who it was. The man, an Englischer, at first stared at Eli and then shifted his eyes away. Eli talked with Mark and told him he and Rebekah were happy about the upcoming wedding. The other man slipped out and the blacksmith greeted Eli.

"I will have this ready for you in a little while if you wish to wait," he said. "It will take perhaps a half hour or so."

Eli agreed to wait. Mark picked up his tool and paid the blacksmith, then left. While the shoe was being worked on, Eli thought of the Englischer who had looked at him with fixed eyes earlier. He must have been thinking the same thing I was as to whether we knew each other or not, thought Eli. Eli had enjoyed a short Rumspringa in his late teens and met a few people in the outside world. Most were friendly but one in particular spoke using crude language and Eli withdrew from him. The man had not taken it well but Eli returned home to his Amish community and thought little more of the man. He now wondered if that was the same man. There was something familiar about his surly face. His thoughts were interrupted a while later when the blacksmith handed him the repaired shoe. Eli thanked him and after paying, he walked across to the General Store to purchase items Rebekah needed. At the last minute he looked at the bolts of fabric. Rebekah loved to sew and it had been too long since she sewed something new for herself.

"Perhaps you can help me pick out some material for Rebekah?" asked Eli.

Mary knew Rebekah well. She smiled and led Eli to the fabric. "I know how much she likes blue. Is that the color she wants?"

Eli said it was to be a surprise for her and he allowed Mary to choose. A soft grayish blue woolen cloth was pulled down. "This may work better than buying cotton. It will be a nice material for the upcoming cold months." Eli agreed and Mary cut the yardage and then wrapped it in white paper. She tied it with a string and handed it to Eli. "She will be surprised," said Mary.

Eli smiled, and happy with his purchase he envisioned the look on Rebekah's face when she saw what he bought for her. He knew at one time Rebekah had hoped to open her own fabric shop. He thought of ways to build the business on their property. They were only a few miles from town and in the middle of the Amish community. Only one other Amish sewing shop existed and it was on the opposite side of the community. It was a very small one and mainly sold to close neighbors to that farm. Tonight he would present the idea to Rebekah during supper.

Eli had approximately one mile to go before reaching home. He was on the shoulder of the blacktop road that led to the dirt road and finally to the lane that took him home. Cars passed him with speed but his horse was used to the movement of the fast-moving machines. He was lost in his thoughts of Rebekah's future sewing shop until he noticed a buggy stopped on the side of the road ahead of him. He pulled over to the shallow ditch as far as possible. A few feet away a fence separated the highway from a field. Eli looped the reins of his horse around one of the fence posts and approached the buggy. Marian Zook stood looking at the front left wheel that sat askew. Her face relaxed when she saw Eli.

"My wheel is broken," she said. "I have no idea what to do, Eli."

"I will take a look," said Eli. He assessed the damage and stood up. "It does not look too bad. I believe I can fix it right here and you can be on your way."

"Oh, danka, Eli. I am so thankful you came along when you did."

Eli bent down and with strong hands shifted the wheel in place. He then went to his buggy and looked inside the small implement box he carried. Retrieving needed tools he returned to the wheel and tightened loosened bolts. He stood and told Marian it was secure. He stepped back to the edge of the shoulder and surveyed his work.

At that very instant, Charles Stenter swerved his car to miss a large rock on the highway. In a flash, Eli was sent spiraling across the ditch. The Englischer gasped, slammed his brakes and jumped out. With his cell phone to his ear he called 911 for emergency help. Marian, whose face was chalk-white, stood in shock at the scene. Several cars stopped to assist. The ambulance arrived in a short time and examined Eli who lay unconscious in the shallow ravine. Charles Stenter stayed close by to the Amish man who did not respond.

"He has a pulse," stated the EMT. "Let's get him out of here and to the hospital." He barked orders to other aides and the ambulance sped off with Eli Stauffer in it. A female police officer approached Marian.

"Are you his wife?" she asked.

Marian shook her head no and in a soft voice she explained why Eli had stopped. Her voice quivered uncontrollably. The Officer brought a blanket from the car and wrapped it around the woman's shoulders.

"Do you want me to take you to the hospital as well and get checked out?" she asked.

"I must get home to my children. My sister is caring for them until I get back," said Marian. "Eli stopped to help me. I do not know what happened after that."

The Officer spoke gently to the woman. "I will take you home and we can get someone to come back for the buggies and your horses. Come now. Everything will be all right."

Just at that moment an Amish couple came upon the scene. The Officer turned to them when they stopped and she explained what had happened. "I do not yet know the man's name but Mrs. Zook told me his first name is Eli. Do you know him?"

"That must have been Eli Stauffer. I saw him in town a little while ago. We will take Marian home and make sure the buggies are retrieved," said the Amish man.

His wife had already gotten out of their buggy and tied the reins of Marian's horse to another fence post. She dreaded giving the news to the

Stauffer family and most of all to Rebekah Stauffer. She looked inside Eli's buggy and took out the items he bought from the store. Then she spoke softly to Marian and her husband helped the widow into their buggy. The Officer decided to stay at the scene, not only to help gather information from the accident but also to guard the buggies until someone came back to get them.

Sarah and John Troyer exchanged glances and John drove the horse to Marian's home.

"I must go and tell Rebekah what has happened," said Marian. "She must know as soon as possible."

Sarah told her to go on in and get a cup of hot tea with her sister. They would go to the Stauffer home and tell Rebekah what had happened.

When Rebekah looked out the kitchen window she expected to see Eli coming up the lane to the house. Instead, she saw the Troyers. Their faces were very drawn when they came to her door. It took everything in her power for Rebekah not to collapse on the floor at the news. John left Sarah with their friend and he hurried to Danny Combs' house. He had a workshop in back of his home where he repaired cars and machinery. When Danny heard the news he quickly washed his hands and got into his car. He headed for the Stauffer home and Rebekah was waiting for him. Sarah took Samuel and she and John then went to the Bishop Daniel and Clara Stoltzfus home to give them the news; from there to Robert and Ruby Stauffer's, Eli's parents.

"We will go back to Rebekah's and pick up things for Samuel," said Sarah to Ruby. "I will take care of him as long as needed, so none of you will have to worry."

Prayers swarmed through the group and praise for Gott's mercy made their way to the heavens. The grandparents nodded their thanks and quickly hitched their horses to the buggies and left for town. The Troyers returned to Eli's and Rebekah's kitchen. Sarah placed the purchases on the table. They left with Samuel.

By evening the Amish community prayed hard for Eli Stauffer's recovery as news circulated fast among them. Jacob Byler dropped everything and reached the bedside of his best friend. He found Rebekah clutching the hand of her husband. Eli had not regained consciousness and her ashen face fixated on him, willing him to respond to her. Jacob knelt by the bedside and began to pray aloud. He asked Gott to bring his best friend back and to allow Rebekah to feel his love again.

The grandparents of Samuel surrounded Eli's bed and prayed with Jacob. Rebekah could not speak. She did not pray at all. No words came to her. A nurse came in and told the family they would have to wait in the nearby waiting room. The doctors needed to run tests on Eli and he must have quiet. The only way Rebekah let go of his hand was for one nurse to unwind it gently and then help her up. Clara came and put her arm around her daughter and led her out of the room. Jacob turned his tear-streaked face away and went to splash water on it before returning to join the family.

Everyone bowed their heads and continued to pray for Eli. The Bishop asked for strength for his daughter. He knew Rebekah felt only fear in her heart. He prayed for her restoration and faith.

CHAPTER SIX

Faith Alone

THE MACHINES' HUMMING overtook all sounds of Eli's breathing. Rebekah could not pray. She spoke to Eli as she held his hand. Her desperation increased when he did not wrap strong hands around hers in return.

"Please, Eli, I need you. Come back to me."

She quietly begged her husband to return to her throughout the night. No one could convince her to leave his side. In the very early morning hours, a nurse told her she must leave. She led Rebekah to a small room that had a cot in it. The mattress was thin but padded. She helped her onto it and covered her with a blanket.

"I will let you know right away if there is any change," she said. "My name is Mable."

Mable had a kind face and when she looked at the young Amish woman her heart went out to her. She overheard her relatives mention someone taking care of the baby. This mother needed her husband and Mable meant to do everything possible to make that happen. Right now, nothing looked good for the patient. He suffered a severe head injury and the doctor ordered diuretics to be administered intravenously. This hopefully would reduce bleeding. Mable passed the small waiting room. The family had left but two Amish couples took their place and prayed as the others had done. She was astounded at the close-knit community that supported each other. Throughout the night the Amish took turns waiting. There still was no change in Eli Stauffer's condition.

Clara Stoltzfus and Ruby Stauffer convinced Jacob to leave when they did. Mable had told them she would take care of Rebekah and see that she rested. Jacob made Mable promise to tell Rebekah he would return early the next morning.

Rebekah awoke and had to focus on where she was. The white wall that held a painting of a garden filled with flowers met her eyes. She slumped back on the pillow when she realized where she was. She then quickly got out of bed and came out the door. She found the restroom down the hall and took time to straighten her kapp and tuck loose strands of hair under it. She splashed cool water on her face and hurried toward Eli's room. Mable had not awakened her which caused her heart to drop. Eli's condition had not improved. She looked up just before Eli's room to see a cheerful nurse approach her.

"Mable's shift ended and she is home. She told me to make sure you were all right. My name is Tracy. I will be here when you need me."

Rebekah thanked her and went in to see wires still connected to Eli. His face was pale and his thick blonde hair was hidden for the most part under a bandage. She sat in the chair at his bedside and spoke to him.

"Eli, please wake up." Tears blurred her eyes. Then she knew what she had to do. "I will pray, Eli. You follow my prayers in your mind. Gott will heal you and bring you home soon."

Jacob heard Rebekah's prayers. Her head was bowed and nearly touched Eli's shoulder. Her hand was clasped around his. Jacob knew today they must both be stronger than they had ever been in their lives. He prayed Gott would heal Eli soon. He turned to see Rebekah's mother come to her daughter.

"Come, Rebekah. I am taking you home for a while. If you do not rest, you will do no gut for Eli. Samuel needs you, too."

Rebekah realized she had not thought about her precious son. She stood up and then turned and kissed Eli. "Come back to Samuel and to me, Eli," she whispered.

The summer air felt good on Rebekah's face. She looked up into the heavens and thought for the first time that her life had changed drastically. When Eli returned home, she knew it would be a long time before he was healed enough to farm and go through his daily life as before. The thought that he would be home was enough for her right now. He must come back, she thought. Clara and Daniel took their daughter to their home. Sarah and John waited there with Samuel.

"Danka to both of you for everything," said Rebekah. She took her son from Sarah's arms. She savored the smell of his soft body. "Samuel has been in gut hands."

Clara moved the cradle next to the table and told her daughter to sit down. The aroma of homemade vegetable and beef soup reached Rebekah. For the first time since yesterday, she felt hungry. Her father sat down and gave a blessing over the food. Rebekah wondered who would care for the farm while Eli was in the hospital.

As if reading her thoughts, Clara spoke. "Jacob and others are taking care of chores at your house. Everyone will take care of things until Eli comes home."

Rebekah was thankful for her close Amish community. She wanted to return to the hospital after lunch but her mother told her to take a nap first. When her head sank into the pillow in her former bedroom, Rebekah was asleep within seconds. After a few hours she awoke to knocking on the back door. She hurried downstairs to meet Jacob.

"I came by to tell you there is no change in Eli. The Doctors will run more tests and hope to give him relief soon," he said. "Rebekah, there is no need for you to go back to town today. It is getting late and you will be more refreshed tomorrow."

She started to disagree when her father spoke. "He is right, Rebekah. Tonight you should spend time with your son. After a complete rest you can go back to Eli's side in the morning."

"If you wish, I can take you and Samuel back home now," said Jacob.

Rebekah felt that was a good idea. She needed to get home again and Samuel needed his own bed. He was beginning to be fretful and she knew it was because of the upheaval in his life the last two days.

When she was settled in Jacob's buggy she grasped how much she wanted to be home again. She tried not to think that when she arrived, Eli would not be there. Faith surged within her that it would be short-lived. Eli would improve and be home any day. Jacob attempted to reassure her. He had seen Eli and his friend's face displayed a more sallow shade. He thought of their boyhood together. They counted on each other for things throughout their lives, even into adulthood. How could he go on without him there? His thoughts switched to Rebekah. As hard as the thoughts of losing Eli were to him, how much more devastating would something like that mean to her.

Jacob carried Samuel inside along with the bag of baby items. Then he told Rebekah he would go ahead and milk the cows while he was there. That proved unnecessary since two young men from a neighboring farm were completing the task when he got to the barn. They talked of other things needed and one climbed to the hayloft and pushed hay down. Once chores were finished Jacob returned to ask Rebekah if she needed anything else done. She thanked him and together they placed milk in the icebox.

"I will have to make butter soon," she said. "I have to admit, Jacob, churning is not a favorite task of mine."

They smiled and Jacob told her he would get Sarah over to do that. The milk needed to be churned since more than usual was in the icebox. They prayed together for Eli before Jacob left. Samuel was fed and nestled in his own bed. Rebekah went into the sitting room and picked up Eli's Bible. She missed their evening conversations. She walked to the window and looked into the night sky. Stars dotted across it. A feeling of peace finally enveloped Rebekah. She sat back down and turned to the passage about

Jesus healing the lepers. Only one came back and thanked him for his healing. Rebekah chose to thank Gott now, before Eli's healing. She knew Gott would work a miracle for her and for her husband.

Once more she gazed at the wondrous skies. The familiar quiet of the farm surrounding her made her think that Eli was there with her in spirit. She must continue forward and keep her own strength up for the sake of Eli and Samuel.

Faith alone gave her unfaltering resolve.

CHAPTER SEVEN

Strength to Live

CRISP WINDS BLEW in as an early warning of fall. Rebekah pulled her wrap around her as she made her way to the barn. A young man from the neighboring farm smiled at her as he greeted her. She thanked him and took one of the milk pails. The warmth of the kitchen would have been a comforting feeling for Rebekah if Eli did not lay motionless in the hospital. Zeke asked if he could do anything else for her and she told him that was everything. Rebekah offered him a hot cup of kaffe which he accepted.

"Rebekah, I know how hard this is for you. Do the doctors think Eli will come home any time soon?" asked Zeke.

"We are trying to work out something to bring him home. We feel family can do as much for him here as in the hospital."

Rebekah was overwhelmed with how much the hospitalization was costing. There was a community fund to help but she felt Eli would not want to take from it unnecessarily. Zeke stood and thanked her for the coffee. He assured her everyone continued their prayers for Eli. After Zeke left, Rebekah bundled Samuel in a woolen blanket and started walking across the pasture to her parents' home. She must talk with the Bishop and Clara. Plans should be made as soon as possible.

Clara opened the door wide to welcome her daughter and grandson. She set two cups of coffee on the table.

"I wish to talk with you and Daed, too," said Rebekah.

When Clara summoned her husband from his small office, the three of them sat at the table.

"The bills are piling up," said Rebekah. "So far, we can pay them but in less than a week we will have to ask for help from the community funds. Eli would not want that." Clara reached for her hand and noted how drawn Rebekah's face was. Her daughter carried a heavy load. Rebekah continued. "Eli has not responded for over two weeks. I believe if he came home to familiar surroundings, he would get better. I want him home with me and with Samuel."

The Bishop agreed with his daughter. They decided to approach the doctor who cared for their son-in-law and find out what needed to be done. "We will stop and ask Ruby and Robert to talk to the doctor with us," said Daniel. "They should have a say in this matter as well."

When they arrived at the hospital, Jacob was sitting at Eli's bedside and praying earnestly. It was difficult for Rebekah to watch. She knew they were like brothers to each other. So far no one close to her husband had succeeded in awakening Eli. Jacob looked up and moved back for Rebekah to talk with her husband. She told Eli the plans to get him back home. The Bishop talked with a nurse and asked to see Eli's doctor.

After agreement from all sides, it was decided that Eli would be going home to continue care there among his family and community. They set the time of discharge for two o'clock that afternoon.

The family was encouraged to get something to eat in the cafeteria while preparations were being made. For the first time since Eli's accident, they had an appetite. As they stood to go back to Eli's room, an Englischer waited for them at the dining room door. He stepped forward.

"I cannot remain silent any longer," he said. "I am the one who caused your husband's condition." He looked at Rebekah. "I am the one, who to dodge a rock, hit him. I am so sorry."

Tears threatened to overflow the man's ruddy face. He was approximately forty years old, lanky and filled with remorse. Rebekah took a step toward him and extended her hand.

"What is your name?" she asked.

"I am Charles Stenter. I saw the buggies on the shoulder of the road but I had no idea when I swerved that I was that close to your husband. I am so sorry."

"Mr. Stenter, you are forgiven. It was an accident and we do not hold blame against you. The woman he stopped to help told us he had stepped back to look at the repaired wheel on her buggy. Eli was at the edge of the highway, though still on the shoulder. None of this was your fault."

Tears flowed down his face. "I have been keeping up with his progress. I want to help you in any way that I can. What can I do for you?"

Rebekah told him of their plans to bring Eli home. She explained his condition had not improved and she thought it would if he were home. Charles Stenter thought it a possibility that the hospital was expensive for the family as well. He mentally thought of one way to help them. The family excused themselves just as a nurse came rushing to them. Rebekah recognized Tracy.

"Come quickly to Mr. Stauffer's room. He is stirring and we think he is coming out of his coma."

In a short time, the family came into Eli's room. Rebekah rushed to his bedside and laid her head on his breast. His breathing sounded more stable and she prayed her thanks aloud to Gott.

"Eli, you are coming back to us. Gott is so gut," she whispered.

Eli smiled weakly and then closed his eyes again.

Two doctors and Tracy moved to Eli. They checked the wires still connected to him. Tracy asked the family to leave the room for a few minutes while they completed the examination. They returned to the small waiting room and prayed together. Jacob exchanged looks with Rebekah. Their eyes glistened with hope. Jacob motioned to Rebekah to come to the hall with him.

"What is it, Jacob?"

"I want to share my joy with you. I feel strongly that Eli will recover and be back to his normal routine soon. Prayer is powerful."

Rebekah nodded in agreement. "I believe he will have a long road ahead of him. He will need to regain his strength. He has lost weight as well." She was already making plans for the next steps to recovery for her beloved Eli. Her heart overflowed with happiness and gratefulness.

Eli deserved to be well again. It would be a matter of time until her family would be restored once again.

Inside Eli's room, his doctor shook his head. The three drew aside from the bed and had a short discussion in low tones.

"We should keep him here a while longer. The bleeding has not stopped completely. If he is coming out of the coma, then he will need other treatments as well. As we know, there will be therapies down the road to consider." The doctor looked at his team. "This is a good sign, but we all know it could have been a fleeting moment for him."

"I hate to see the Amish family get their hopes up too high," said Tracy.

"They have a strong faith. Who knows whether that will restore him to complete health again or not?" said the second Doctor. "I have seen miracles before when I gave up hope on a patient."

They nodded in agreement. Tracy returned to Eli's bedside and spoke to him. She was positive that he could hear his family's prayers and voices. "You are strong, Eli. You can get well. Just hang in there," she told him.

CHAPTER EIGHT

The Father's Arms

THE STOLTZFUS AND STAUFFER FAMILIES, along with Jacob Byler were elated at the awakening of Eli. The Bishop and his wife made the decision to return home. All agreed to wait a while before taking Eli home from the hospital. The doctor had explained everything to them, and cautioned them to not get their hopes up too high. This did not faze the family. They knew the doctors had skills to heal people, but more than that, there was a Gott above them who had the final say.

Word spread of Eli's improvement. He had regained consciousness three more times for short periods in the next three days. Church services the next Sunday were at the Bishop's home. The congregation obviously felt relief and thanksgiving for their neighbor.

"Eli is strong," said one woman. "He will be home and well again soon."

The others spread out the food on the tables and agreed with her. The young men and women were cheerful and talked of Eli and Rebekah. Everyone loved the young family. Most of them had attended the schoolhouse together when younger. Nancy had visited Eli several times but she chose to spend as much time as possible with Rebekah when she was away from his bedside. Rebekah was overjoyed at the support everyone gave her. It only quickened her faith in Gott and his healings.

Rebekah was pleased that Marian Zook did not look as sad about the accident as before.

"Jacob, do you think Eli will be home soon?" asked Nancy. She stood alone with him to talk. Rebekah left to return to the hospital. "Rebekah is very hopeful."

"I do not know, Nancy. I have to say that I sometimes wonder if he will make it or not. When he awakens, it is for brief moments. The nurse, Tracy, told Rebekah that he is attempting to speak. That is a gut sign."

He looked out across the pasture to the Stauffer home. Once it had been filled with life. Eli and Rebekah planned to have more children to fill the home. Something told Jacob that it may never be that way again. He shook his head to rid negative thoughts. Nancy looked at him closely. Her heart skipped a beat with fear.

"What is it, Jacob?"

"I do not know why this feeling came over me. We must praise Gott for his mercy and love over us all."

He bowed his head and began a prayer. Nancy did the same. Both thought there could not be any answer except healing for their close friend. Laughter and conversations flowed in the background. No matter what, the Amish community continued to prove to be their extended family. Jacob knew that Rebekah returned to the hospital by herself. She left Samuel with her mother and told them she would be home before dark. The wind picked up but did not account for the cold feeling that rushed over Jacob.

"I am going to town. Will you please let the Stauffers know? Tell them I will stay by Eli's bedside with Rebekah. Perhaps we can bring him back to us completely before the day is over."

Nancy stood back as Jacob whirled around and walked quickly toward his buggy. Her heart sank at the possibility that Eli would leave them all. She recalled the fond memories they shared as children. She whispered a prayer and went to locate the parents of Eli. They had left for home and she found them sitting in their kitchen sipping hot tea and coffee.

Ruby smiled at Nancy and invited her inside to join them. Nancy told them that Jacob and Rebekah would remain with Eli until evening. "They hope to help him to become more alert."

"It is in Gott's hands," said Robert. "We must not worry. Whatever His plans are will be ours as well."

When Jacob got to Eli's room, he stopped and looked at his two friends. As much as he still loved Rebekah, he only wanted his best friend to be healthy again. Eli and Rebekah were the perfect couple. They matched well and were meant for one another. He must get well, Jacob said to himself.

He listened to Rebekah's voice. "Eli, the cut of material you bought me is perfect. I love the color and the wool is so soft. What made you think to do that for me? I love you so much. We will have evenings together while I sew my new dress. You will think it is lovely when I am finished with it."

Eli's eyes fluttered and then opened. Rebekah's heart beat faster. Eli smiled in appreciation of his wife. He listened for days to her voice while at his bedside. At times, it slurred into meaningless mumbling and was hard to know her words. He was aware she was at his bedside. She told him of their precious son and his progress. She reminded him of his plans to teach Samuel everything he knew about farming. She assured him that everyone helped at their farm. Not everything she said to him made sense. He was sure her voice wavered at times. He did not want her to cry for him. When he came to, he was already making plans for her, though at times even his thoughts lost track of one another.

Eli Stauffer knew he would not return home and resume life as he had known it. At times, his head pounded with pain and then he had no idea of his surroundings at all. He recalled an Englischer visited him. Was that someone he knew in his past? He could not be sure and so far he struggled to make his voice work again. He wanted to express his thoughts to Rebekah with words. He wished for the strength to grasp her delicate hands as in the past.

Now, Rebekah turned from him and told Jacob to come in. At last, thought Eli, my beloved Fraa and my best friend, my true bruder, are here together and alone with me. I must force my voice.

"Rebekah," said Eli. She quickly turned back to him. His voice was raspy and she was not sure if he said her name or not. He repeated it in a whisper. "I love you, my Fraa, my beloved."

His words were measured and he closed his eyes as if in exhaustion. Then he opened them and looked at Jacob. His hand moved toward him and with drained energy he motioned for him to lean toward him. Rebekah moved back and Jacob leaned down. Eli's hand slowly guided him to turn his head so he could tell him something.

"Take care of Rebekah and my child," he whispered.

The halting words were pronounced. Jacob nodded and told Eli he should not worry. Then Rebekah's gasp made Jacob turn to her. Mable had just come onto her shift and stood at the door as Eli breathed his last breath. She wrapped Rebekah in her arms and signaled for help.

CHAPTER NINE

Awakening

FOR REBEKAH, THE next months left her carrying out chores and duties to her son as if she walked in a dream world of her own.

One day when she looked through the window at the rising sun she knew as if awaking from a dream that she must resolve to go forward without Eli. Their son needed her. He was walking now and each day he resembled his daed more and more. The day Rebekah looked at Samuel and laughed for the first time was the day he followed her to the barn with his own small milk pail.

"If your daed cannot show you how to milk a cow, then it is up to me, little one. Samuel's eyes glistened in the sunlight that peeked between the clouds. He looked up and pointed to emerging fluffy white ones. They parted for the sun to come into its own position for the new day.

"Milk," said Samuel. He stumbled as he looked into the sky.

Rebekah laughed at her son's word. "Ja, it is milk. Let us show your daed what a big boy you are with that milk pail."

Samuel dropped it twice until Rebekah paced her steps with his. She must show her son how to keep milk pails clean before squirting milk into them. Eli had been right. There was much for their son to learn about the Amish way of life. Rebekah knew Samuel would be the man he was meant to be just as Eli had been the man he was meant to be. Faith alone allowed peace to restore itself once again within her.

When they finished the milking lesson, Rebekah took Samuel's pail as he ran ahead of her. The clip-clop sound of a horse was heard before she saw the owner of the buggy. Jacob stepped out of it and smiled at her. She thanked Gott that Eli's best friend had faithfully come to help her with harvesting and general farm chores she could not do by herself.

Jacob did not push Rebekah. He promised Eli he would take care of her and Samuel. He did not waver from his intention to keep that promise. In Gott's gut time, he thought, He will lead us all in the right path.

***

THE END

Following the shocking death of Eli, Rebekah and her small son, Samuel, must fall upon their faithful God, and close friends and family, more than ever before. Her story continues in the next book in this warm series, *Love's Promise*

You can also enjoy the first chapter of Love's Promise right now. I have included it as a BONUS at the end of this book. Enjoy!

CHAPTER TEN

Read Them All

THE ANGELS AMONG US SERIAL is a beautiful journey. Join Rebekah through the joys and challenges and see God's love work on her behalf…

The Bishop's Daughter

Faith Alone

Love's Promise

Hope Renewed

The Testing

Song of Life

Home Truths

Amish Light

CHAPTER ELEVEN

Bonus Chapter – Love's Promise

Chapter 1 – An Unexpected Visitor

REBEKAH STAUFFER PRAYED early in the morning for strength to meet another day on her own. She ran her fingers over the railing of the bed Eli carved for their son. Samuel's face emitted a peace she only recently discovered again within her own being. Rebekah had accepted Eli was in heaven with their Gott and she could no longer pine for him. This was harder to do on some days than others. She thanked her Gott for the support of her family and her community. Most of all, she thought about how generous Jacob Byler had been in keeping up the farm. Jacob promised Eli he would take care of Rebekah and Samuel. Eli whispered this wish to his best friend before taking his last breath.

"I am coming, Samuel," said Rebekah. She was thankful her son awoke each day with a smile on his face.

Just as she picked him up, she heard a knock on the door. She did not expect Jacob until later in the morning and was curious who it could be. She saw a male figure through the light crisp kitchen curtain and hurried to the door.

"Mrs. Stauffer, I am Richard Blanton. I hope I do not disturb you," said the man.

She wondered how he knew her name. There was something about the tall, slim man that seemed familiar to Rebekah but she could not place where she may have seen him before. He was an Englischer though he reminded her of an Amish man because of his mannerisms toward her.

"How may I help you?" asked Rebekah.

"I am passing through and I am looking for a way to earn money so that I may continue my journey. I understand you are a widow. I felt that you could use some help on your farm."

"My community helps me and I am sorry but I have no need to hire anyone," said Rebekah. A slight shiver ran through her body. Never before had she known an Englischer to seek a job in the Amish community. "I am sure there are odd jobs available in town for you to look into."

Samuel began to cry and she glanced back at him now sitting in his high chair. In his baby talk he demanded food.

"I am sorry," said Rebekah, "but I must go now. I hope you find a job if that is what you want."

She breathed deeply when the man turned from her, and she closed the door behind him. She gave Samuel a cracker to keep him happy while she prepared breakfast for both of them. Once the meal was finished and her kitchen cleaned up again, she picked up Samuel and headed toward the barn. He wiggled until she let him down to walk with her. She paced her steps to meet the toddler's. The morning was clear and sunny. Neighbors, along with Jacob, had planted corn in the acreage near the barn. She stopped and shielded her eyes to survey the even rows.

Inside the barn, she handed Samuel his small milk pail. He happily stood next to Rebekah while she began to milk the cow.

"Be sure and get the pail in the right place," she said. He nodded his head and she squirted milk a few times into his pail and then filled her own from the two cows. Each time one pail filled, Samuel's eyes lit up. Teasing him, Rebekah told him to open his mouth and she squirted milk between his soft lips. He squealed in delight. When they returned to the kitchen, Rebekah showed him how to pour the milk into jars and set them into the icebox. Lifting Samuel onto a stool by the counter she grasped his small hands and helped him pour from his pail into a jar of his own.

"You are a gut kinner," she said. Her next chore was to clean the house. She pulled the sheets tight on her bed and ran her hand across Eli's side of the bed. Samuel tugged on the blanket, mimicking his mother. "I hear someone coming, Samuel."

She hoped the Englischer had not returned and felt relief when she recognized her mother. She and Samuel ran to greet her. Clara Stoltzfus beamed at her daughter and grandson. She knew Rebekah healed more each day and she hoped her daughter would soon marry again.

"I came to help you today," said Clara. She placed an applesauce cake on the table.

"Danka, Maemm. I am sure you have plenty to do at your own haus," said Rebekah. "First let us have a cup of kaffe." She poured two cups for them and Samuel pointed to the icebox. Rebekah laughed. "He just milked the cow and wants the milk from his own jar," she said.

Once they were settled, Clara talked of things she heard in the neighborhood. "I do not want to upset you, but some have seen an Englischer walking back and forth on our road." Clara noticed a look of alarm on her daughter's face. Bishop Daniel and Clara Stoltzfus lived across the pasture from Rebekah. They shared the same road as well as other close neighbors.

"He was at my door early this morning," said Rebekah.

"What did he want?"

Rebekah told her mother of the strange request from the stranger. "I have no idea how he knew my name or how he knew I am widowed. That is most mysterious of all."

She went on to tell Clara that during the short conversation, she thought there was something about him that reminded her of their Amish men.

"He could have belonged to an Amish community at one time," said her mother.

Both women knew that on rare occasions when a young person left for his or her Rumspringa they chose not to come back home. It was unusual, but it did happen. Rebekah had not thought about that as a possibility.

"It could explain why he thought an Amish person would hire him. Maybe he is familiar with our way of life."

Rebekah thought it an explanation but was uncomfortable that the man named Richard Blanton knew so much about her. She decided to change the subject and asked her mother if she wished for another cup of coffee. Clara told her if they kept drinking coffee they would never get the chores done. Her mother wanted to talk with her daughter about remarrying before the morning was over. She and Rebekah's father, the Bishop, did not think it was a good thing for her to remain alone much longer. Now that the stranger knew who Rebekah was concerned Clara. She was surprised when Rebekah brought up the subject of marriage herself. It was almost noon and they were making roast beef sandwiches for lunch.

"I will eat with you since your Daed has gone to the next community. He is meeting with two Preachers there today." Bishop Daniel Stoltzfus was available to surrounding ministers in the Amish communities. They valued his leadership.

Rebekah was more than happy to have company for a meal. She loved having Samuel there but she became lonely talking to a two year old all the time. She pulled a macaroni salad from the icebox and set a large pitcher of iced tea on the table. Clara placed the sandwiches next to them. They were laden with mayonnaise, pickles and lettuce. Rebekah grilled a toasted cheese sandwich for Samuel and placed a pickle and chopped bits of roast beef on his plate. She filled his glass with milk.

"I have been thinking a lot, Maemm," said Rebekah. "It is difficult living alone. I must finally let Eli go and look for a gut husband again."

"I am so happy to hear you say that. There is someone very close to you who would be a very gut husband for you." Clara's eyes twinkled. "He comes every day since Eli died and waits for you patiently."

"Are you speaking of Jacob?"

Clara nodded. "He has spoken with your Daed. He has been in love with you since before you married Eli. Can you find love in your heart for him?"

Rebekah leaned back. How could she have missed that? Jacob did everything for her. He once told her he promised Eli he would take care of her and Samuel. For the first time, Rebekah wondered if Eli had meant for him to do more. Did he mean he wanted Jacob to marry her and take care of her the rest of her life as husband, and father to Samuel?

She voiced her thoughts to her mother. "I know that Eli whispered something to Jacob before he died. Jacob later told me he asked him to care for me and Samuel. Do you think Eli meant for Jacob to marry me?"

Clara smiled. "That is the way Jacob Byler took it all. He has been very patient all these years. He did not resent Eli marrying you. He accepted that you were meant for one another. Now he feels you are nearing the end of your deep grief over Eli's death and he is ready to marry you."

Rebekah looked at her mother and smiled. "I have not thought about Jacob more than a very gut friend. But now that the subject comes up, perhaps I have been in love with him these last few months."

They heard a horse and buggy approach the house. Clara smiled to herself when Rebekah spoke with new life in her voice. "It is Jacob. He told me he would be late this morning."

Clara gathered her plate and rinsed it from the water pitcher near the sink. "I will leave you two alone. I am sure Jacob will be hungry."

Rebekah barely noticed when her mother walked past her and greeted Jacob outside. She remembered to thank her for her help, but Rebekah's eyes were on Jacob Byler.

Pick-up a copy of Love's Promise by Grace Given to continue reading.

ABOUT THE AUTHOR

Grace Given is an author of sweet, Christian Amish Romance.

For as long as I can remember I have been fascinated by the simplicity and faith of the Amish people. In a world so busy and self-consumed, the virtues of a simple life are more and more appealing to many people.

Amish romance has given me the opportunity to express my own heart's desire for a world less cluttered, where love and virtue abound.

Thank you for choosing a PureRead Romance. As a way to thank you we would also like to give you a special novella, Grace Abounding.

http://pureread.com/gracegiven

OTHER BOOKS BY GRACE GIVEN

SWEET ROMANCE
Homeward Bound
Timeless Amish Love Stories
Angel's Among Us
Abrams Child
Angels Among Us Series

ROMANTIC MYSTERY
Amish Assault On The Highway
Stranger In The Woods

Thank you so much for reading.

READ ALL OF GRACE'S BOOKS

pureread.com/gracegivenbooks